D0964328

Hello. If I have been silly enough to mislay this diary please return it to:

Mr. Bean
c/o Mrs. Wicket
"Daffodils"
12 Arbor Road
LONDON N10

A £5-00 reward would certainly not be out of the question.

The number of i's on this page is 53 56 57 64

First published in the UK in 1993 by
BOXTREE LIMITED,
Broadwall House,
21 Broadwall,
London SE1 9PL

20 19 18 17 16 15 14 13

Text copyright © Tiger Television, 1993
Photographs copyright © Tiger Television, 1993

Designed by Nigel Davies for Titan Studio.
Photography by Paul Forrester.
Reproduced by Positive Colour Ltd.
Printed and bound in Great Britain by
Bath Press Colour Books, Glasgow

Front cover photograph of Mr Bean courtesy of
Stephen F. Morley.
Back cover photograph of Mr Bean courtesy of
Thames Television.

A catalogue record for this book is available from the
British Library.

ISBN 1 85283 349 1

my place

Mr. Bean's

HIGHBURY DISTRICT COUNCIL DIARY

So watch it

Compiled for the H.D.C. by
Robin Driscoll and Rowan Atkinson
of the National Diary, Calendar and Phases of the Moon Office
at the Department of National Heritage

B⬚XTREE

HIGHBURY DISTRICT COUNCIL

Mayor
Sarah Mahaffy
32 Tongdean Rise,
London N5

Councillor
Nichola Motley
Housing Committee
Broadwaters,
308 Waldergrave Rd,
London N5

Councillor David Inman
Planning Committee
29 Duchland Avenue, London NW8

Councillor Susan Cole
Environment Committee
Flat 3, 21 Downlands Close, London N9

Councillor Chantel Noel
Women's Committee
c/o Highbury Town Hall

Councillor Rod Green
Policy Committee
c/o Highbury Town Hall

Councillor Adrian Sington
Emergency Committee
Church Villas, 15 Dukes Road, London N5

Councillor Elaine Collins
Equal Oportunities Committee
4a George Street, London NW4

Temperature Conversions

°C	°F		°C	°F		°C	°F		°C	°F		°C	°F		°C	°F
-20	-4.0		1	33.8		22	71.6		43	109.4		64	147.2		85	185.0
-19	-2.2		2	35.6		23	73.4		44	111.2		65	149.0		86	186.8
-18	-0.4		3	37.4		24	75.2		45	113.0		66	150.8		87	188.6
-17	1.4		4	39.2		25	77.0		46	114.8		67	152.6		88	190.4
-16	3.2		5	41.0		26	78.8		47	116.6		68	154.4		89	192.2
-15	5.0		6	42.8		27	80.6		48	118.4		69	156.2		90	194.0
-14	6.8		7	44.6		28	82.4		49	120.2		70	158.0		91	195.8
-13	8.6		8	46.4		29	84.2		50	122.0		71	159.8		92	197.6
-12	10.4		9	48.2		30	86.0		51	123.8		72	161.6		93	199.4
-11	12.2		10	50.0		31	87.8		52	125.6		73	163.4		94	201.2
-10	14.0		11	51.8		32	89.6		53	127.4		74	165.2		95	203.0
-9	15.8		12	53.6		33	91.4		54	129.2		75	167.0		96	204.8
-8	17.6		13	55.4		34	93.2		55	131.0		76	168.8		97	206.6
-7	19.4		14	57.2		35	95.0		56	132.8		77	170.6		98	208.4
-6	21.2		15	59.0		36	96.8		57	134.6		78	172.4		99	210.2
-5	23.0		16	60.8		37	98.6		58	136.4		79	174.2		100	212.0
-4	24.8		17	62.6		38	100.4		59	138.2		80	176.0		101	213.8
-3	26.6		18	64.4		39	102.2		60	140.0		81	177.8		102	215.6
-2	28.4		19	66.2		40	104.0		61	141.8		82	179.6		103	217.4
-1	30.2		20	68.0		41	105.8		62	143.6		83	181.4		104	219.2
0	32.0		21	69.8		42	107.6		63	145.4		84	183.2		105	221.0

[Handwritten annotations: "BRR!", "MMMMMMMMMMM NICE" down the first column; "PHEW! SIZZLE OUCH! DEAD" down the third column; letters "D E A A D" across upper columns; letter "E" repeated.]

Conversion Values

Distance

miles to kilometres	1.6093
yards to metres	0.9144
feet to metres	0.3048
inches to millimetres	25.4
inches to centimetres	2.54

Area

square miles to square kilometres	2.59
square miles to hectares	258.99
acres to square metres	4046.86
acres to hectares	0.4047
square yards to square metres	0.8361
square feet to square metres	0.0929
square feet to square centimetres	929.03
square inches to square centimetres	645.16
square inches to square millimetres	6.4516

Volume

cubic yards to cubic metres	0.7646
cubic feet to cubic metres	0.0283
cubic inches to cubic centimetres	16.3871

Capacity

gallons to litres	4.546
quarts to litres	1.137
pints to litres	0.568
gills to litres	0.142

Speed

miles per hour to kilometres per hour	1.6093
feet per second to metres per second	0.3048
feet per minute to metres per second	0.0051
feet per minute to metres per minute	0.3048
inches per second to millimetres per second	25.4
inches per minute to millimetres per second	0.4233
inches per minute to millimetres per minute	2.54

Mass *[handwritten: → 10.00 St. Marys]*

tons to kilograms	1016.05
tons to tonnes	1.0160
hundredweights to kilograms	50.8023
centals to kilograms	45.3592
quarters to kilograms	12.7006
stones to kilograms	6.3503
pounds to kilograms	0.4536
ounces to grams	28.3495

[handwritten: HEEHEEHEEHEE]

Mass per Unit Area

tons per square mile to kilograms per square hectare	3.923
pounds per sq. foot to kilograms per sq. metre	4.8824
pounds per sq. inch to grams per sq. centimetre	70.307
ounces per sq. foot to grams per sq. metre	305.152

[handwritten: STUPID]

Mass per Unit Length

tons per mile to kilograms per metre	0.6313
pounds per foot to kilograms per metre	1.4882
pounds per inch to kilograms per metre	17.858
ounces per inch to grams per millimetre	1.1161

Fuel Consumption

gallons per mile to litres per mile	2.825
miles per gallon to kilometres per litre	0.354

Addresses & Telephone Numbers

The Queen
Buckingham Palace (Flat No.?)
London
ENGLAND

Ex directory

Inspector Morse
Oxford, Nick
Oxfordshire

999

Prime Minister
10 Downing Street
London   (Weekdays)

071 290 3000

Chequers   (W/ends)

0945 482451
(PayPhone — Pub

Shirley Bassey
On my Wall
In my room
My House
My Street
ENGLAND

081 467 8290

KILL KILL
KILL
KILL

GOD
Everywhere (literally, apparently)

Crematorium
That place in the trees with
the chimney

081 858 5010

Mum
Clapham Cemetery

Shovel Store 071 736 5926

Grandad
~~Tree Grove Road~~
~~LONDON N4~~
(Moved in with Mum)

December

Xmas '92

Oooh! Diary for Christmas

3pm Queen

26 Saturday

↑

Boxing Day?

27 Sunday

↑↑↑↑

??

Still no sign of Boxing Day

December

8 Monday   Boxing Day !/////

~~Dear Mrs. Queen~~
~~Dear Eliz~~

Dear The Queen
I hope you are well. I am fine. A most peculiar thing
~~has happened.~~ You may remember that last year Boxing
Day was on the day after Christmas, and most properly so.
Why oh why ~~oh why~~
     Ever since ~~Napoleon that man~~
     ~~Napoleon~~ Bonaparte was never blown apart ☺

11:00 Corner Shop
     PILCHARDS

9 Tuesday

9.00 Hospital → 291 2777
     Tell Doctor: Both ends went in the night
         Pilchard?

December

30 Wednesday

12.00 Pie in
12.25 Pie out

31 Thursday

Put the slippery soap
On the slippery slope

NEW YEAR
RESOLUTIONS

1. Become Millionaire
2. Tidy room.
3. Buy other slipper

27. Marriage

Set alarm for 12.00 midnight

1 Friday

A brand spanking New Year
Clean and shiny and
sparkling and lovely

1993

GLINT
GLEAM

DURA GLIT

SHIRLEY BASSEY
9.00 Ch 4 ?!!
10,000 watts

2 Saturday

3 Sunday

January

4 Monday

9.40 Buy new swimming Trunks.

11.00 Try Trunks (POOL)

5 Tuesday

10.00 Report Police Station (re. Trunks
coming off)

(Letter of Apology)   TO: St. Bernadette's School for Girls.
Hampstead Road London NW1

Dear ~~Lorna~~ Headmistress
Can't apologise enough for awful
incident in front of your young women ~~the was~~
~~of an~~ My ~~to her way than~~

4.00 POST BOX

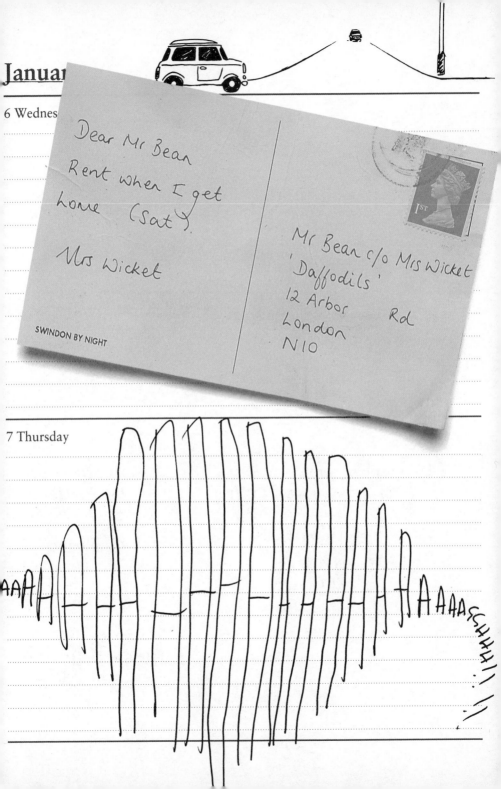

Januar...

6 Wednes...

7 Thursday

January

8 Friday

4.00 Bottom Problem

9 Saturday

7.45 Keep Fit with
thin woman (ITV)

9.00   20 Press Ups
  20 Sit Ups
  20 Pull Ups
  20 Jump Ups

10 Sunday

9.00   20 Press Ups
  20 Sit Ups
  20 Pull Ups
  20 Jump Ups

That one with the fat
girl 8.00
BBC2

11 Monday

9.00 ~~20~~ 10 PRESS UPS
~~20~~ 10 SIT UPS
~~20~~ PULL UPS
~~20~~ JUMP UPS   10.00 LIBRARY

Try to get: "GUNS OF NAVARONE"

"HIS BODY WAS IN BITS"
by Zak Brood   CLIFF

"DEATH IS FREQUENTLY UNEXPECTED"
(Z. Brood)

12 Tuesday

9.00 4 ~~20~~ PRESS UPS
4 ~~20~~ SIT UPS
4 ~~20~~ PULL UPS
4 ~~20~~ JUMP UPS

2.30 Go back and peek
at Librarian
(re. Marriage)

Wobble Dobble Fobble Bobble

January

13 Wednesday

9.00 20 PRESS UPS
      20 SIT UPS
      20 PULL UPS
      20 JUMP UPS

10.00 Peek at Librarian?

Irma Something

14 Thursday

9.00 20 PRESS UPS
     20 SIT UPS
     20 PULL UPS
     20 JUMP UPS

NO NO
NO
NO
NO NO
NO OOOOOOO NO
NO

15 Friday

9.00 20 Press Ups
      20 Sit Ups
      20 Pull Ups
      20 Jump Ups

HATE HATE

Mr. Muscles ←

16 Saturday

17 Sunday

10.30 Visit Mother

← 22 along →

9 down

MUM

N
W   E
S

January

18 Monday

Ring Irma Gobb

(Library 658 4890)

19 Tuesday

12.15 Lunch in PARK

12.25 Leave Park (Too much Poo)

4.00 Shops: Carpet Shampoo
Pott Pourri

9.15 Park

STILL too much Poo in Park

DOG DEVICE

CORK

© Mr. Bean

21 Thursday

Ring Inspector Morse

January

22 Friday

Dear Inspector Morse
There's so much poo in our Park you
wouldn't believe it. Can you come and investigate?

I will gladly help you. I have a good ~~set of~~
set of spanners

Mr. Bee Bee Bean

---

23 Saturday

That loud one with
the beard 630 ITV

24 Sunday

Vicar out all day

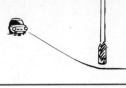

25 Monday

10.00 Library ♡

Take book: Guns of Nav.
2 x Z. Brood

Take out: "Gone with the Wind" (ROMANCE)

"Stand and Deliver"
(Autobiog. of Mollie Saxton, Midwife)

"His blood ran freely" by Zak Brood

26 Tuesday

MR. BEAN

invites you to a Party at

The Park (near Coin-Op Toilets)

DISASTER
IF WET

BRING A SANDWICH
(TWO IF YOU'RE FAT)

Send to
Irma

January

27 Wednesday

4.45 Ring Irma Gobb

Put Cat out ~~of its misery~~

28 Thursday

4.45 Ring Gobb

January

29 Friday

1.30 Wash Spanners

4.45 Get Gobb

30 Saturday

Irma Gobb
Has got a Job
In a busy Library
She does her Job
(Does Irma Gobb)
In a library north of Highbury
Irma Gobb
Who's got this Job
Somewhere north of Highbury
Is the same old Irma Gobb
Whose hands are thin and fibrey

31 Sunday

February

1 Mon

→ Romance?

8.10 Take Irma Gobbto
Pictures

2 Tuesday

Bob a Bob
Joba Bob

Gob A Gob A Gobble Gobble

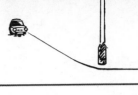

February

3 Wednesday

9.00 Ring Gobb

10.00 Ring Gobb

11.00 Ring Gobb

12.00 Ring Gobb

1.00 Ring Gobb

Where is Gobb?

---

4 Thursday

8.30 Ring Gobb	11.30 Ring Gobb	2.30 Ring Gobb
8.45 Ring Gobb	11.45 Ring Gobb	2.45 Ring Gobb
9.00 Ring Gobb	12.00 Ring Gobb	3.00 Ring Gobb
9.15 Ring Gobb	12.15 Ring Gobb	3.15 Ring Gobb
9.30 Ring Gobb	12.30 Ring Gobb	3.30 Ring Gobb
9.45 Ring Gobb	12.45 Ring Gobb	3.45 Ring Gobb
10.00 Ring Gobb	1.00 Ring Gobb	4.00 Ring Gobb
10.05 Ring Gobb	1.15 Ring Gobb	4.15 Ring Gobb
10.30 Ring Gobb	1.30 Ring Gobb	4.30 Ring Gobb
11.00 Ring Gobb	1.45 Ring Gobb	4.45 Ring Gobb
11.15 Ring Gobb	2.00 Ring Gobb	5.00 Ring Gobb
11.30 Ring Gobb	2.15 Ring Gobb	5.15 Ring Gobb
		6.00 Ring Gobb
		6.15 Ring Gobb
		6.30 Ring Gobb

February

HATE HATE
HATE
HATE
HATE HATE
HATE
HATE HATE
HATE HATE
HATE

HATE

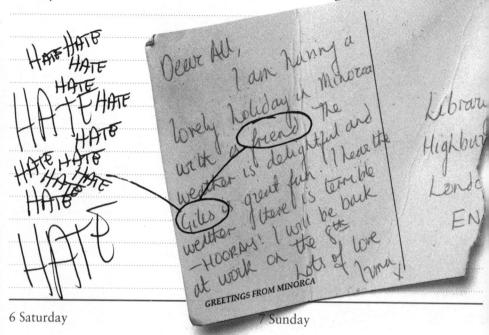

Dear All,

I am having a lovely holiday in Minorca with a friend ~~Giles~~. The weather is delightful and great fun. I hear the weather there is terrible —HOORAY! I will be back at work on the 8th

Lots of love
Emma x

GREETINGS FROM MINORCA

Librar
Highbur
Lond
EN

10.00 Smiths Do-It-All
~~Either~~ Sniper Rifle
OR Rope
Sheath Knife
Strichnene
Mousetrap?

February

8 Monday

Hurt Flay Rip
Slash Gouge
Hit
Stab

If I put a bomb under Giles
He will go for miles and miles
And miles and miles and miles
and MILES

† GILES ↑HEAVEN ✗
↓HELL ✓

9 Tuesday

VeNGeANCE
(with hangman figure)

9.30 Crimewatch UK BBC1
(Ideas)

February

10 Wednesday

2.45 Report to
Police Station

METROPOLITAN POLICE
RECEIPT

your ref:

our ref:

Surrendered Goods

1 BRNO .22 AIRRIFLE
1 10" KNIFE
1 SMOKE CANISTOR
3 MOUSE TRAPS
1 lt. ARALDITE
10 m. ROPE

P.C.R.Leavis

The above items have been confiscated pending
a decision by local magistrates

Go to bed
ZZZZZZZZZZZZZZZ
11 Thursday Wake up

2.00 — 2.10 Sunny

I love P.C. Leavis
x
x x

February

2 Friday

Buy ~~Grow beard~~ NO
Fudge YES ✓✓
✓✓
✓✓✓

---

13 Saturday

Roses are red
Violets are blue
You were Miss Gobb
And I was Mr.

Got the ~~doo~~
Spew the ~~doo~~
For man choo
Who got the ~~doo~~
The ✓

14 Sunday St Valentine's Day

No card

Samaritans
071 2367425

10.00 Put Out Bin

February

15 Monday

16 Tuesday

February

7 Wednesday

18 Thursday

February

19 Friday

20 Saturday

21 Sunday

2 Monday

3 Tuesday

February

24 Wednesday

FOUND DIARY!!

25 Thursday

Hiphip hoozar
Hiphip haha
Yippee Yippee Bippee
Bippee

1.15 Soup

HAPPINESS

5 Fr ay

N o 3.

Dear Mr Bean,
We havn't met yet but
I have just moved into N°3
down the hall. Enclosed is
your diary which I found
today by the bins in the porch.
I would very much like to
call to make your aquaintance
and perhaps to pick up the
reward you mentioned on
the first page?!
Man in
N°3. SPM

Avoid Man in
No. 3

7 Saturd

N.B. Man in No.3   N.B. Man in No.3

March

1 Monday

Shops: Farty Cushion
False Dung
Funny Hat
Celery

Those two men in that house 8.30 ITV

AVOID

IN

2 Tuesday

March

Wednesday

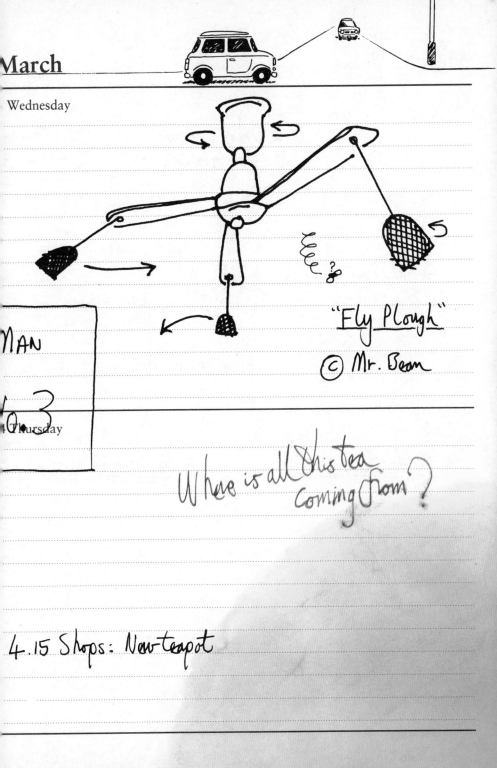

"Fly Plough"
© Mr. Bean

MAN
3

Thursday

Where is all this tea coming from?

4.15 Shops: New teapot

March

5 Friday

9.00 N.B. Order Flowers
         for Grandad ✓ ⟵

2.00 Ring Grandma AAARGH!

RING FLORIST
RING FLORIST

Funny Man with wart 10.00 ITV

6 Saturday

9.00 RING FLORIST

7 Sunday

9.00 RING FLORIST

Monday

GRANDAD's 90th BIRTHDAY (QUITE AMAZING REALLY)

RING FLORIST : CHANGE MESSAGE

3pm Grandad Funeral

9 Tuesday

Send off for Shirley Bassey Mug (Large)
to: Shirley's Mug (Large)
P.O. Box 203
Swindon
Wilts. SN43 7PZ

"PORTABLE PHONE"

© Mr. Bean

March

10 Wednesday

3.00pm Ring Irma Gobb — leave funny noises
on Answering Machine
(sobbing?)

11 Thursday

PINK TICKET NO. 77

KEEP IT SAFE

Draw: 27 March

GRAND RAFFLE

In Aid of Police
Benevolent Fund

1st Prize:
A Week
in the Bahamas

2nd Prize:
Dinner for Two at Pizza Hut

Friday

THE FLOWER

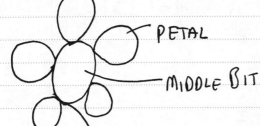

PETAL

MIDDLE BIT

7.30 Botany Club

Saturday | **14 Sunday**

LEAF

OTHER LEAF

GROUND

LITTLE ROOTS

ROOTS

WORM

March

15 ...nday

could end up esca...
for a week somewhere.

VIRGO
(Aug 22nd -
Sept 22nd)
It could be time to retile
that bathroom. You will
receive shattering news
on 27th March, possibly
regarding the number 77.

LIBRA
(Sept 22rd -
Oct 23rd)
All your money worries will
end soon when you get a
big windfall, possibly from
the pools

GOOD OMEN OR WHAT?

12 DAYS TILL

RAFFLE

16 Tuesday

8.15 Rajpoot Tandoori
(Table for One)

March

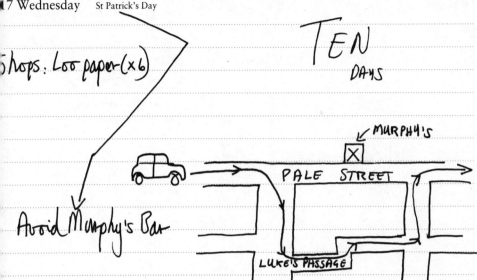

17 Wednesday — St Patrick's Day

TEN DAYS

Shops: Loo paper (x6)

MURPHY'S

PALE STREET

Avoid Murphy's Bar

LUKE'S PASSAGE

18 Thursday

NINE DAYS

FRAZZLE
FRAZZLE

JACKET

BAHAMAS

"RAFFLE PRIZE"

© Mr. Bean (no copycats)

March

19 Friday

EIGHT DAYS

10.30 Building Society
Take all money out
Put no money in

Holiday shopping: Shirts
                    Socks
                    Biscuits ✓
                    Vaseline

                    Marmalade?

---

20 Saturday

SEVEN DAYS

Buy holiday shoes

---

21 Sunday

SIX DAYS

NO shops open
NO shopping
(except Vaseline)

OATH OATH OATH!

Corydalis Lutea

March

22 Monday

FIVE DAYS

4.15 Buy holiday shirts

23 Tues

FOUR DAYS

2—4.45
Holiday shopping spree spree spree spr

March

24 Wednesday

3

Buy holiday socks ✓

25 Thursday

2

Ring Building Soc
— no money

Buy holiday celery ✓

If $\triangle + @ + !!! + \sim = \circledast$

and $\pi + \otimes - \boxed{\odot} = \triangle\equiv$

What is $\boxed{\odot}$?

MAD MAD
MAD MAD

(4 APRIL)

26 Friday

1

...AL CHECKLIST: MOSQUITO STUFF
FILM
CROCODILE KNIFE
SNAKE GREASE
SPOON

Buzz

ooh!

Buy holiday underpants
(both types)

---

27 Saturday

0.55 Cross Fingers

1.00 RAFFLE
DRAW
St. Andrew's Church
Hall

BLAST OFF

28 Sunday

Travel to
Barbados
on plane

March

29 Monday

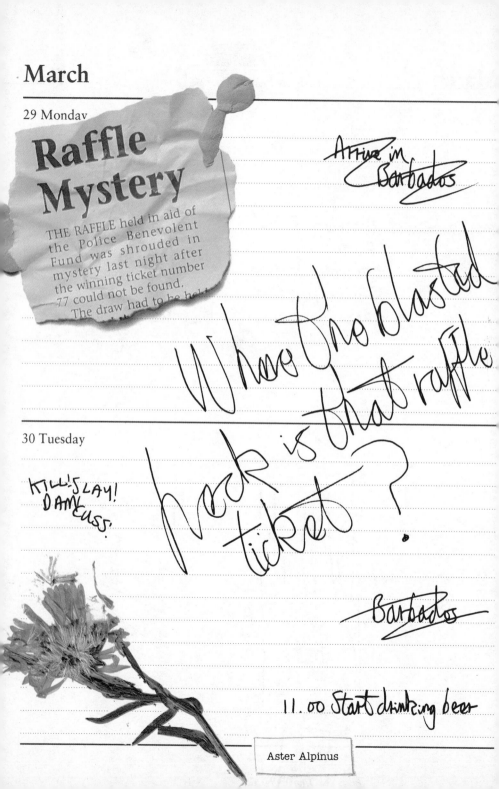

Raffle Mystery

THE RAFFLE held in aid of the Police Benevolent Fund was shrouded in mystery last night after the winning ticket number 77 could not be found. The draw had to be held

Arrive in Barbados

Where the blasted is that raffle ticket?

30 Tuesday

KILL! SLAY! DAMCUSS!

Barbados

11.00 Start drinking beer

Aster Alpinus

March/April

31 Wednesday

Drink beer all day

Barbados

POLICE Station Help

Samaritans
2367925

↓ and all night

1 Thursday   April Fool's Day

Barbados

11.45
N° 3.

Dear Mr Bean,
A parcel arrived
for you while you
were out. I have
it with me.

Man in N° 3.
(down hall).

11.15 Man out —
try later

2.10 No Man

4.42 No Man

April

2 Friday

~~Barbados~~

Where oh WHERE is Shirley Bassey mug ?

Ring Swindon.

D. Plumb
Private Investigator
799

Try man in No. 3

7.30 ~~Botany Club~~
Too depressed

3 Saturday

~~Barbados~~

~~Send back~~ Cliff Richard
mug. GET OUT CLIFF
COME IN Shirley
WHERE ARE YOU ??

4 Sunday

~~Barbados~~

$$\boxed{O} = \boxed{} + \acute{O}$$

Try man
in No. 3.

Monday

Dear Mr. Plumb

I am distraught beyond measure. I have lost a raffle ticket No. 77 and I don't know where to put myself or what to do. I have lost all sense of direction and have forgotten how to make tea, even with a tea bag which is so simple really, isn't it? I last saw the ticket in my hand on March 17th. I don't know where it is. I'm sure I put it somewhere but now somebody called Caroline has gone to Barbados.

Tuesday

HATE
HATE HATE HATE

CAROLINE

Snakes → ssss s
ssssss

Ring Samaritans 236 7925
re. Raffle Crisis

NO ESCAPE

PLAN VIEW

April

8.30 Banana

Barbados

N° 3.

Dear Mr Bean,
I know you have been
knocking on my door,
but I have been ignoring
you because there _is_
no parcel!

APRIL FOOL!!

6.00 No Man

Man in N° 3
(down hall).

8 Thursday

Bonfleet 8N8

April

9 Friday   Good Friday

6.15 Steal Milk (No. 3)

Barbados

Send back Des O'Connor mug.

SEEDS: ~~Pansies~~ NO   Nasturtium ×
Deadly Nightshade   ⟨7.30 Botany Club⟩
Widow's Misery ✓   Love Lies Bleeding ✓

---

10 Saturday

Barbados

10.10 Goringe's (seeds)

11.00 Plant seeds

8.10 All About Terrapins
(David Attenborough)
BBC2

11 Sunday   Easter Day

Boiled Egg

Seeds growing

April

12 Monday   Easter Monday

Terrapin Budget:

Glass tank   £69 — 95   Seeds Growing
Water   £ 0 — 00
Filter   £ 15 — 95
Heater   £ 25 — 50
Gravel   £ 8-00 from shop
                £ 0 — 00 from next door's drive
Weed   £ 2-50 from shop
                £ 0 — 00 from next door's garden
Terrapin   £ 0 — 20p ↑ CHEAP

13 Tuesday

I love
Mr. Bean

Seeds Growing

Terry the
Terrapin

April

14 Wednesday

Shirley Bassey mug
arrives HOORAY!!

Seeds growing

1.00 Lovely hot steaming mug* of Tea mmmmmmmmmmmmmmmmmm!

15 Thursday

Seeds still growing

10.15 Pet Shop – buy Terrapin

3pm Christening (of Terry)

* Shirley Bassey type, large

April

16 Friday

This makes me so cross

Seeds growing?

17 Saturday

10.00 Check Seeds

Oh, bottoms

18 Sunday

Seeds RUINED
(DOG)

April

9.15 Buy seeds
9.45 Sow seeds

Sow seeds: Monkey Flower ✓   Red hot poker ✓✓
Baby's breath (UURGH)   Stinking Helibore ✓

~~Devil in a bush~~ stupid

Plant seeds

5.45 am Creep out and steal milk

Seeds growing

Ring Samaritans
(keep them talking)

← RUDDY MOUSE
PRINTS

April

21 Wednesday   Queen's Birthday   Ring?

(New) Seeds should still be growing

"Mousetrap Mk. 1"

© Mr. Bean

22 Thursday   5.50am Sssssssssshhhhhh Steal more milk

Wossit
Grossit
Twissit
Fossit

Seeds growing

That really funny one   7.00 Ch. 4

April

23 Friday

10.00 Check seeds

To sum up:
1. Nothing happening
2. No little green bits.
3. No flowers.
4. No nothing.
5. No good

CUSS CUSS
CUSS CUSS
CUSS

SEED MAN —

SNAP !

25,000,000,000
000,000,000,000
000,000,000,000
000,000,000,000
TONS

24 Saturday

Nº 3.

Dear Mr Bean,
Milk bottles are
frequently stolen
from outside my
door. Can you
throw any light
on the matter?

Man in Nº 3
(down hall).

25 Sunday

He must be really stupid

April

26 Monday

Yabadabadabadabadabadabadabadabadabadabadabadabadabadabadabad OOO!

→ .

27 Tuesday

That grimly man who was in that old Police programme with Inspector Morse and ran off with the leggy dancer

8.30 BBC1

To Mr Boon

Yours,
Shirley Bassey

April/May

If you make a jelly in a teapot
And try to slop it out
It takes about a fortnight
To get it out the spout

---

1 Saturday

Mayday mayday
All around
Ship in fog
Big hooting sound

All that noise and fuss
you make
keep it down
For goodness sake!

2 Sunday

Write to Shirley
Bassey re. her
lovely mug

(v. v. v. v. v. v. v.
v. v. v. important)

Monday   May Day

"FOOT REST"
© Mr. Bean

Tuesday

-3 Give us an S	S	Give us an o	O
Give us a T	T	Give us a .	.
Give us a u	U	Give us a 3	3
Give us a p	P		
Give us an i	I		
Give us a d	D		
Give us an m	M		
Give us an a	A		
Give us an n	N		
Give us an i	I		
Give us an n	N		
Give us an n	N		

What is that spell?

STUPID MAN

IN No. 3

May

5 Wednesday

6 Thursday

Highbury District Council
Council Offices
Highbury, London N10

Mr Bean,
c/o Mrs Wickets,
Daffodils,
Room 2, 12 Arbor Road,
London N10

15th May 1993

Dear Mr Bean

Thank you very much for your letter of the 5th May concerning, as you see it, the "outrageous" shape of your toilet.

Unfortunately, the obligations of your local council extend only as far as the provision of sewage facilities in the borough, and we cannot be held responsible for the shape of any individual apparatus. Certainly the shape of the pan you describe (your drawings are returned herewith) would appear to be traditional.

I was naturally distressed to hear of the effect that this "mad toilet" is having on your mental health. Your nightmares, accompanied, as you claim, by the "banshee howls" akin to the sound of "two enmeshed chainsaws (two-stroke)" would only become the responsibility of the local authority if complaints were received from other tenants at Daffodils. This department has no record of any such correspondence.

I therefore cannot entertain your request for a Community Charge rebate, merely on the basis of the "horrifying scenes" you describe, and the blame which you directly attribute to the curvature of your lavatory.

Yours sincerely

G.M. Nuttall

May

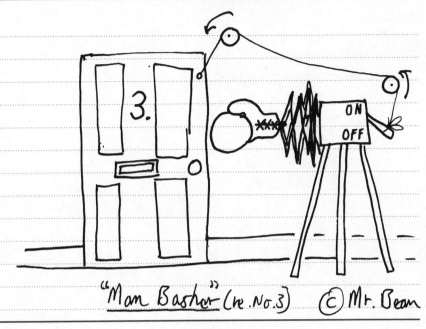

"Man Basher" (re. No.3)   © Mr. Bean

Saturday

TEE HEE HEE

9 Sunday

9.15 Rubbish

10.00 More Rubbish

May

TON

← CHICKEN SOUP.

10 Monday

Hello Monday you look nice and fresh, but
then you're always the first day aren't you?

11 Tuesday

Oh Tuesday goodness me
You've come along too, how delightful.
How do you do?

12 Wednesday

ooopp! Gave me a bit of a fright, that Wednesday although I should have expected you, I know, because you always bowl up on Day 3.

Sit down, do.

I've got some bitter lemon if you'd like some but nothing alcoholic I'm afraid (burp)

Oh, and Wednesday this is Thursday.

13 Thursday

Oh, you've met, I'm sorry. You met last week?

How interesting!

Silly me.

May

14 Friday

FRIDAY where have you been?

I've been so anxious. You're always so late, you naughty boy, the week's nearly over. Honestly.

15 Saturday

Brr Brr. Brr Brr.
Ting.

Hello? Yes Mr. Beanhive. Can you not make it Saturday? But it's the sixth day, and you're expected. Oh tish pish posh.

16 Sunday

The Lord's Day

(not my responsibility)

May

17 Monday

THE GROCER (Caught Unawares)

Blancmange

Stonehenge

Nothing rhymes with Orange
Except perhaps Lozenge.

18 Tuesday

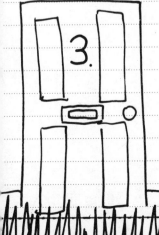

3.

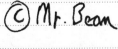

© Mr. Bean

CARROT

May

19 Wednesday   8.15 Get up.

Ring Irma Gobb

Join Poetry Class 7.30
(Ms. Rosemary
Hasebury)

10.30 Go to bed

20 Thursday   8.15 Get up

If I had a newt   Poetry research: Buy daffodils
I'd have a pursuit.   Ring T.S. Eliot

9.30 Go to bed

May

21 Friday

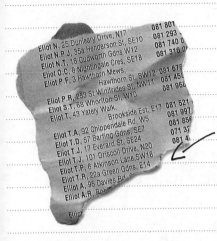

Eliot N, 25 Dunleary Drive, N17   081 801
Eliot N.P.J, 35a Henderson St, SE10   081 293
Eliot N.T, 16 Cudworth Gdns W12   081 740 0
Eliot O.C, 8 Nightingale Cres, SE18   081 316 0
Eliot P.F, 3 Hawthorn Mews,
     Hawthorn St, SW12   081 675
Eliot P.R, 253 St Winifrides St, NW11   081 455
Eliot S.T, 68 Whoriton St, W10   081 968
Eliot T, 43 Yately Walk,
     Brookside Est, E17   081 521
Eliot T.A, 92 Chippendale Rd, W5   081 997
Eliot T.D, 57 Barfing Gdns, SE7   081 85
Eliot T.J, 17 Everard St, SE24   071 37
Eliot T.J, 101 Driscoll Drive, N20   081 4
Eliot T.P, 6 Atkinson Lane, SW18
Eliot T.R, 22a Green Gdns, E14
Eliot A, 95 Davies Rd
Eliot A.R, Rob

Eliot

T.S. Eliot ex-directory?.

10.30 Go to bed (Boring)

22 Saturday

9.30 Get up (Yippee!)

23 Sunday

Don't get up

If I haven't got up then I won't have to go to bed. HOORAY!

10.30 Go to bed.

May

24 Monday

Ring Inna Gobb
And keep it clean
If you get
Answer machine.

Shirley Bassey in Pro-Am Golf   8.00 BBC2

25 Tuesday

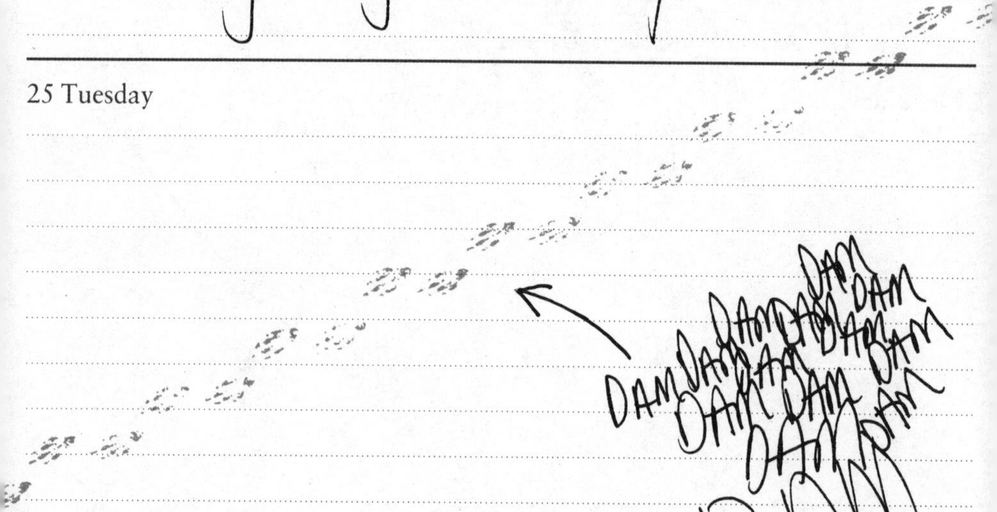

DAM DAM DAM DAM DAM
DAM DAM DAM DAM
DAM DAM
DAM

6 Wednesday

Poem: <u>ATTENTION MICE</u>

You'd better watch out
Cos if I see you about
You're going to end up in my mincer
Then, no mucking about
I'll scrape you all out
And do the same thing to your sister

7.30 Poetry Class

7 Thursday

"<u>MOUSETRAP MR.2</u>"

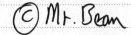

© Mr. Bean

May

28 Friday

9.00 Buy Fish

Leave out all day

29 Saturday

Leave out all day

30 Sunday

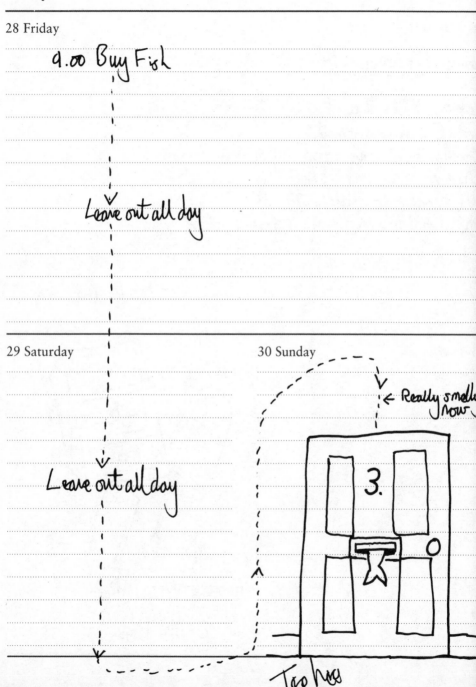

← Really smells now.

3.

Tee hee

1 Monday

Up at nine
Out by ten
Drive to town
Drive home again

Those two men in that house 8.00 ITV

1 Tuesday

HOUSEFLY

FILTH

"HOUSE FLY TRAP"

© Mr Bean

June

2 Wednesday

Picnic shopping : Tea Bag
Lettuce
Sticklebacks in Brine

1.00 Picnic in Park.

Cilla Black
Has a lack
(but) Shirley Withey
Is a cuddly girley

7.30 Poetry Class   (Bassey)

3 Thursday

Don't do ANYTHING today AT
ALL

except go to the toilet

4 Friday

Terry (the Terrapin) R.I.P.

Oh Lord who giveth and taketh away, taketh away Terry and put him in a nice big tank in heaven and remember to feed him because I forgot

Amen.

5 Saturday

Give Terry's tank, water, weeds, and gravel away to somebody —

→ Oxfam?

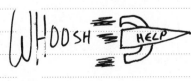

6 Sunday

Help on it's way

WHOOSH ≡ HELP

OFF

June

7 Monday

There's a poetry test
I'm sure to pass
In Ms Rosemary Rosebury's
Poetry Class
She's given us the title
"A Goddess Sublime"
Which will take no time
For the Prince of Rhyme (to do)

8 Tuesday

POETIC LICENCE
ALL
CATEGORIES

EXPIRES: 7 JUNE 1994

Mr BEAN   MALE

9.45 Turn in

9 Wednesday

A GODDESS SUBLIME   by Mr. Bean

If there's anything in the world
That I would like to be
It's Shirley Bassey's microphone
So she could sing to me

I know she sings to everyone
When they come to hear her
But front row seats cost fifteen quid
And I would be much nearer.

Another thing that strikes me   7.30 Poetry Class

10 Thursday About being up that close

Is that I could smell her perfume
And see right up her nose*

I know microphones get dribbled on
But so what, what the hell?
It is a perk of the job when it's Shirley's gob
And I'd get in free as well!

*N.B. Check with Ms. Hosebury — close & nose rhyme

June

Poo-ee!

Ring Samaritans
re . drains

12 Saturday

13 Sunday

11.15 Forget it

Get up early tomorrow

CRASH!

une

4 Monday

11.10 Give blood

5 Tuesday

Dear ~~Council~~
   ~~Nurse Gibby~~,

Wash out
Jam Jar

Dear Blood Man / Woman

I would like to become a blood donor and enclose, for
your perusal,

Highbury Royal Infirmary
Highbury, London N10

re: 16 June
from: Highbury Royal Infirmary

Dear Mr Bean

Although we are pleased that you have decided to become a blood donor, I'm afraid that we cannot accept donations by post. We have disposed of your blood in accordance with the conditions of the Medicines Act 1709, and your jam jar is returned herewith.

Perhaps you would like to give blood when a mobile unit visits your area? If you would like further information, please see your doctor.

Perhaps you will be seeing your doctor anyway?

Yours sincerely

Jose Manteras

Jose Manteras
Doctor

CRASH!

8 Friday

"GRISTLE MASTER"

© Mr. Bean

19 Saturday

Shops: Loaf
Butter
Egg (x2)
Spindle
Grommet

20 Sunday

June

21 Monday

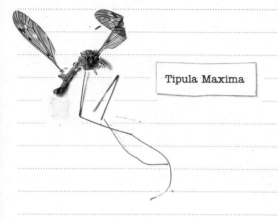

Tipula Maxima

6.00 Lance Boil

22 Tuesday

9.15 Lance Boil

6.15 Ring Lance Boil

7.45 Entymology Club
↳ What is Entymology?

CRASH!

June

Morning: Go to Library

...*uus -uus* f. *integer*: see ENTIRE]
...*e* /ɪnˈtaɪt(ə)l/ *v.tr.* **1 a** (usu. foll. by *to*) give (a
person etc.) a just claim. **b** (foll. by *to* + infin.) give
(a person etc.) a right. **2 a** give (a book etc.) the title
of. **b** *archaic* give (a person) the title of (*entitled him
sultan*). □□ **entitlement** *n.* [ME f. AF *entitler*, OF
entiteler f. LL *intitulare* (as IN-², TITLE)]
entity /ˈentɪtɪ/ *n.* (*pl.* -ies) **1** a thing with distinct
existence, as opposed to a quality or relation. **2** a
thing's existence regarded distinctly. □□ **entitative**
/-tətɪv/ *adj.* [F *entité* or med.L *entitas* f. LL *ens* being]
ento- /ˈentəʊ/ *comb. form* within. [Gk *entos* within]
entomb /ɪnˈtuːm/ *v.tr.* **1** place in or as in a tomb. **2**
serve as a tomb for. □□ **entombment** *n.* [OF *entomber*
(as EN-¹, TOMB)]
entomo- /ˈentəməʊ/ *comb. form* insect. [Gk *entomos*
cut up (in neut. = INSECT) f. EN-² + *temnō* cut]
entomology /ˌentəˈmɒlədʒɪ/ *n.* the study of the
forms and behaviour of insects. □□ **entomological**
/-məˈlɒdʒɪk(ə)l/ *adj.* **entomologist** *n.* [F *entomologie*
or mod.L *entomologia* (as ENTOMO-, -LOGY)]

← BINGO!

ANGRY IRMA

TEE HEE HEE
HOO HEE

June

25 Friday

11.00 MFI (Cupboard - self assembly)

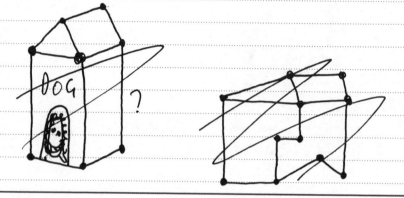

26 Saturday

27 Sunday

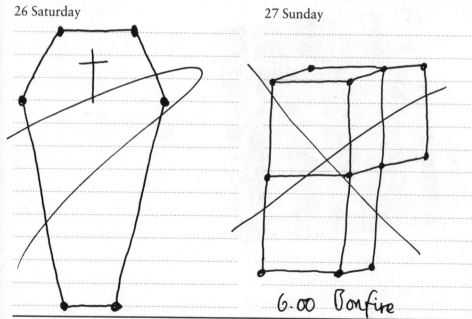

6.00 Bonfire

June

28 Monday

Oh what a horrible morning oh what a horrible day
I've got a horrible feeling that people just get in my way

but only ONCE

and then its

CURTAINS

29 Tuesday

For them

Heh heh heh heh heh
heh heh heh

Yesterday up on the stairs
I caught a man unawares

I gave him a fright again today
By taking both his ears away

(You should have seen him)

7.45 Entymology Club
(Spelling 10/10)

June/July

30 Wednesday

6.00 News (BBC) De de dom de de dommm de de dum
dum dum dum dos dos dos dum dum dos dos dim dommmmmm..
...This is the Six O'clock News from the BBC with thingummy Jig
and what's her face........ de de dom de de dumm.

1 Thursday

Tenebrio Molitor

10.00 News at Ten (ITV)
(Pay attention)

July

Friday

Shops: Shake 'n Vac

12.00 Clean Jacket (Tweed)

3 Saturday

9.20 Go out
10.04 Come in
10.24 Go out again
12.10 Come in again
1.45 Go out again
2.05 Come in again
[2.55 Go out again.
[2.56 Come in again
[2.57 Go out again
4.50 Come in again
6.03 Go out again
6.43 Forget to come in again
7.00 Miss Programme
7.28 Eventually come in again

4 Sunday

CANCELLED

July

5 Monday

Ring Irma Gobb?

No, can't be bothered.

I would very much like to go to the moon, even though I don't like travel, as a rule. No language problems, and no crowding.

6 Tuesday

Also, no air.

GASP GASP GASP

9.10 Over the moon about something

7.45 Entymology Club lots of creepy crawlies

Wednesday

horrible

Young people with ~~funny~~ accents   5.40 BBC1

Thursday

Shopping (to service car): GREASE
                           OIL
                           EGG WHISK
                           $ Filter
                           Coffee
                           G Hitches
                           Spotting spigot

                           Fairy liquid
                           Alarm clock?
                           Bottle   (dont lose it)

July CAR SERVICING
(PHOTO GUIDE)

9 Friday

STUFF REQUIRED

ENGINE
(LOCATION OF)

10 Saturday

CHANGE FILTER

TOP UP RADIATOR

CRASH!

CHANGING THE OIL

TOUCH-UP PAINTWORK

BEFORE

AFTER

ALL DONE!

CHANGE BULB IN BOOT

Entymology Club 7.45

July

14 Wednesday

OLD Getting dressed procedure: First Shirt
then Socks
then Underpants
then Trousers
then Shoes
then Tie
then Belt
BORING then Jacket

15 Thursday

NEW Getting dressed procedure:

First Shirt
then Jacket
then Tie

First Shoes
then Socks

stupid

First Trousers
then Undies
Impossible
-stupid
-barmy

First Belt
then Tie
then Shoes
then Leave House

Too rude

then Jail

First
then
then Undies
Jacket
Tie

Mad mad mad

July

16 Friday

10.45 Library   Return   "Gone with the Wind"
                                "Stand and Deliver"

                  Get out   "Insects of Yesteryear" by E. Dalton

                        "The Land of Gore" by Zak Brood
                        "Limb from Limb" by Zak Brood
                            (Parts 1 & 2)

                        "Are you bleeding comfortably?"
                                (Z. Brood)

also Ask Gobb to Pictures

---

17 Saturday   **18 Sunday**

                                       10.15 Vicar (Exorcism)

6.10 HORROR FILM

                                       Sleep with light on

Seek
Professional
Help.

**North London
Technical College**
Highbury, London N10

Mr Bean,
c/o Mrs Wickets,
Daffodils,
Room 2, 12 Arbor Road,
London N10

16th July 1993

Dear Mr Bean

I'm sure that I need not reiterate the horror and revulsion felt by all of us when you revealed your pressed insect collection. It is inhuman to murder God's creatures in this way, merely to form a macabre collection in the pages of your diary.

There has been a unanimous decision taken by our sub-committee to report your behaviour to the RSPCA, from whom I hope you will be hearing soon.

You really are a quite revolting man.

Dr. Legge
Sec., Entomology Club

CRASH!

July

21 Wednesday

Seek Professional Help re. Nightmares

Z

GGAAAA GH

Can't sleep

22 Thursday

Can't sleep

Clossiana Euphrosyne

July

23 Friday

Smiths Do-It-All : 1 Mirror
: 1 Wooden stake

Sainsburys : 10 lbs Garlic

Sleep with light on

24 Saturday

25 Sunday

8.30 Holy Communion
9.30 Family Service
11 am Mattins

Lock door
Sleep with light on

6.30 Evensong
(Attend religiously)

CRASH

26 Monday

Stay in all day

Breathe quietly

loo: The Exorcist

SSS SSS SSSSssshhhhhhhhhh ---

27 Tuesday

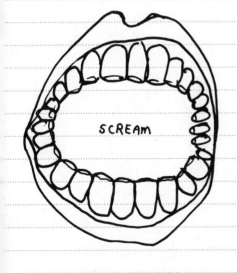

SCREAM

Pull myself
together.

July

28 Wednesday

Close my eyes
up tight and sing
Go away
You big bad thing!
Open them again
And shout

GO A WAY

29 Thursday

NEW SECURITY ARRANGEMENTS

GE

0 Friday

6.00 Shirley Bassey
Master Chef

or you'll

31 Saturday

1 Sunday

A CLOUT!

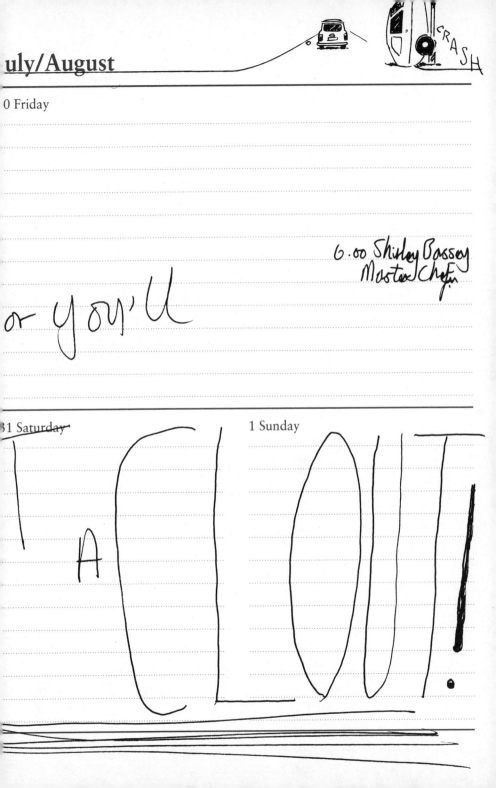

August

2 Monday

Feeling much better today, thank you.

Shops: Beans
Bread

Long Johns

3 Tuesday

9.45 Mrs. Wicket (Root)

7.15 Bum something
(Mrs. Wicket?)

Wednesday

Significant disturbances.

Beans for dinner
Beans for tea
Oh windy Bean
Oh windy me

5 Thursday

Further disturbances (Bottom Dept.)

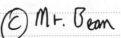

HONEY

© Mr. Bean

August

8.30 Take Mini to Mum

A. & G. MOTORS
10 Ugly Street, Twickenham
081 851 1590

Dear Mr Bean

I thought you should know, that your mini is a Dog. We looked at it this morning. and it is completely clapped. You need a new sub frame mate and big ends and mounts and exhaust etc to name but a few. Tires are as bald as that swimmer bloke. We're talking a lot of cash. like two or three hundred also the brown stuffs everywhere (you been driving fast again !!!!!!!) No I mean the rust its terrible the car is really shot. My feet went through the floor at Sainsburys roundabout, Fred Flintstone Eat your heart out !!! Come to the garage and you better say what you want cos we're going to Rimini Tuesday

Graham
P.S. My mate thinks you're weird

CRASH

9 Monday

"HANDY ASH"

© Mr. Bean

10 Tuesday

12.00 Park

Dear ~~Highbury's~~ Council Man

The state of the park is very outrageous and, in a way, cataclysmic, it is so smelly. I know I may have contributed to the aroma myself recently, because as you may know, I have had my own problems, but the poop is the matter that i

August

'ANTI-DRIP'
© Mr. Bean

11 Wednesday

"Daffodils"
12 Arbor Rd.
LONDON N10

BEAN ANTI-POOP ASSOCIATION (BAPA)

Dear Resident,
    I hope you are well. I am fine. I am writing to
ask if, like me, you are sick and tired of too much poo.
Dogs, treat this road, and the park, like a huge toilet,
which it isn't. Join 'BAPA, and help me stamp out poop.
Any dog owner caught ~~fouling our paths~~ allowing a dog
to foul our paths will get a right dressing down, and
further abuse.

12 Thursday

    Those responsible for more than one poop will
get a punch up the bracket. (We could take it in turns)

If you are interested, please fill in this form, and send it
back.

— — — — — ✂ — — — — —

NAME . . . .
ADDRESS . . . .
. . . .
. . . .

I think your idea is great. Signed .
. . . .

CRASH

13 Friday

9.45 Library (Photocopies). nf. Too much poop (BAPA)

Ring Samaritans
    re. poop.

14 Saturday

15 Sunday

Do I like Golf?

IN →

August

16 Monday

BY APPOINTMENT TO
HER MAJESTY THE QUEEN
POOP PREVENTATIVE AND DIRT DISPOSAL
MERCHANTS BEAN ANTI-POOP ASSOCIATION

17 Tuesday

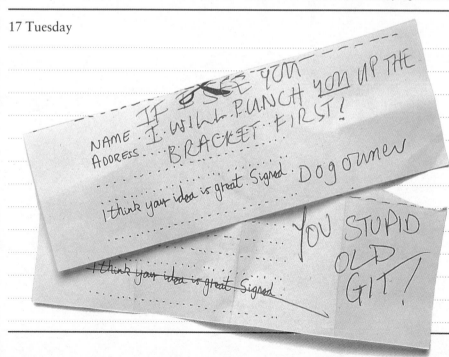

NAME ..... IF I SEE YOU I WILL PUNCH YOU UP THE BRACKET FIRST!
ADDRESS .....

I think your idea is great. Signed. DOGOWNER

YOU STUPID OLD GIT!

I think your idea is great. Signed.

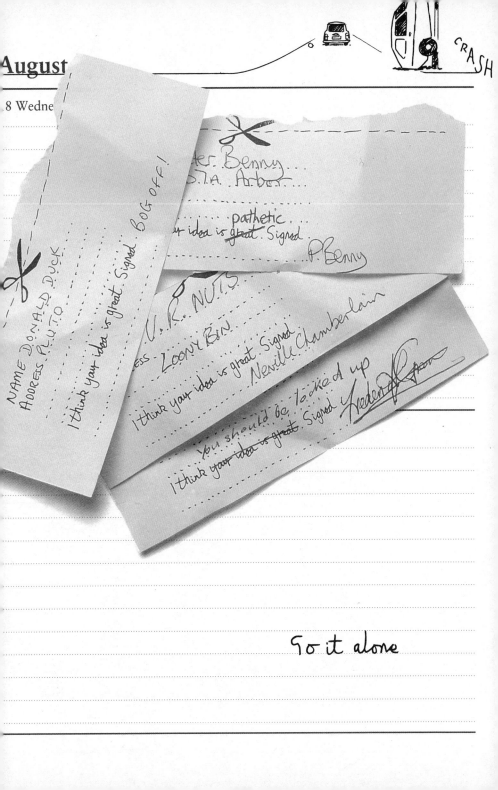

CRASH

NAME DONALD DUCK
ADDRESS PLUTO

I think your idea is great. Signed.. BOG OFF!

..ter Benny
..S.7.A. Arbor

..r idea is great. Signed. pathetic

P. Benny

..ess U.R. NUTS

LOONY BIN

I think your idea is great. Signed.
Neville Chamberlain

You should be locked up

I think your idea is great. Signed.

Go it alone

August

METROPOLITAN POLICE
4, Guildford Street
Highbury
London N10

Dear Mr. Bean

It has been drawn to our attention that you have been circulating letters to the residents in your area of the borough, complaining about the problem of dogs fouling the pavement. This is not a criminal offence in itself, but the blatant incitements to violence which are also contained therein most certainly are.

We received a complaint from a dog owner yesterday, claiming that he was recently attacked by a man answering to your description. After the complainant's pet had made an accidental deposit in the park, the attacker attempted to force the owner's nose into the excreta. This is not the kind of behaviour that upstanding citizens should have to suffer. The hooligan was also carrying a quantity of corks, with one of which he attempted to violate the dog.

If this attacker was yourself, you must appreciate that the Constabulary takes a very dim view of this kind of behaviour: if we hear of any similar incidents, or af any further letters, criminal proceedings will be brought against you.

Yours sincerely

Sgt. Rickers

Sgt. P.R.D. Rickers

CRA

3 Monday

9.00am Commence BAPA Stealth Deterrent Mk. 1

Glue   Tow bar
Soup   Pillow-case
Timber 24' x 1½" x 1½"   Electric Fan
Duvet Cover   Bed sheet
Broom handle   Screws
Bread Knife   Nails
                                 Horse Poop (½ Ton)

---

4 Tuesday

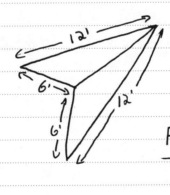

Fig.1

The fat man with the long hands 6.30 BBC1

August

25 Wednesday

Sore throat

I've got to be firmer
with Irma
If she's going to be
A long termer

Nose getting blogged

26 Thursday

Nose completely stuffed
Full of snot.

Chemist: Paraffin
Pipe cleaners?

4.00 Unfortunate snot accident (Mrs. Wicket)

7 Friday

Letter of Apology (Mrs. Wicket)

BAPA Detonant: Fig. 2

28 Saturday

Construction to continue apace.

9.00 Bonk bonk bonk

2.30 Tap tap tap tap

8.15 Kersplak kersplak

29 Sunday

7.00 Bang bang bang bang

bang bang bink OWW!

Bang bang bang

August

30 Monday

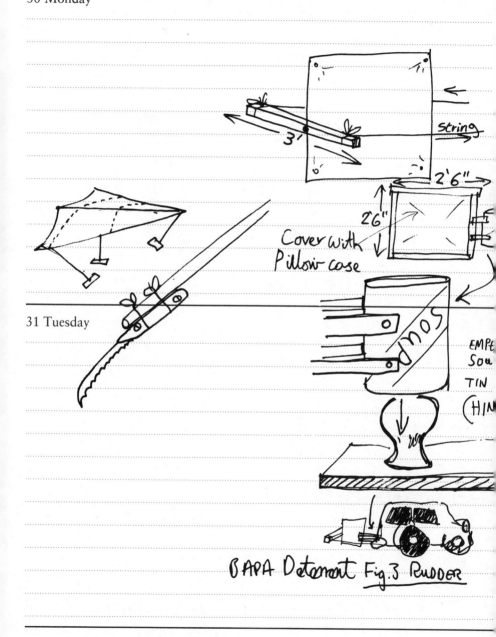

31 Tuesday

String

3'

2'6"

2'6"

Cover with
Pillow case

EMPE
Sou
TIN
(HIN

PAPA Detonant Fig. 3 RUDDER

Wednesday

MRS. WICKET IN BRIGHTON

10.00 Clear Drive
10.30 DELIVERY OF HORSE POOP

2 Thursday

Morning: Fill Duvet Cover with horse poop.

Recipe Idea : RABBIT STEW
2 Pts. Hot Water
1   Rabbit
1   Plate
1   Knife
1   Fork   Boil, Serve, Eat

September

3 Friday

Shops: More screws
Bigger screws

N.B. Need to change Traffic Light sequence, Junction of Arbor Road + New Road

Requirements: Screwdriver
Pliers
Mini
Brain on
full Alert

4 Saturday

Saturday Night's the night for fighting.
(Stay in)

5 Sunday

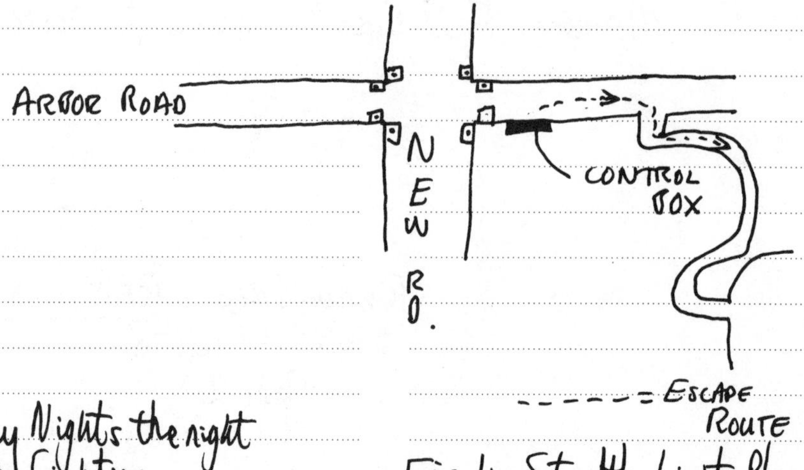
ARBOR ROAD
NEW RD.
CONTROL BOX
- - - - - - = ESCAPE ROUTE

Fig 4 Stealth Lights Plan

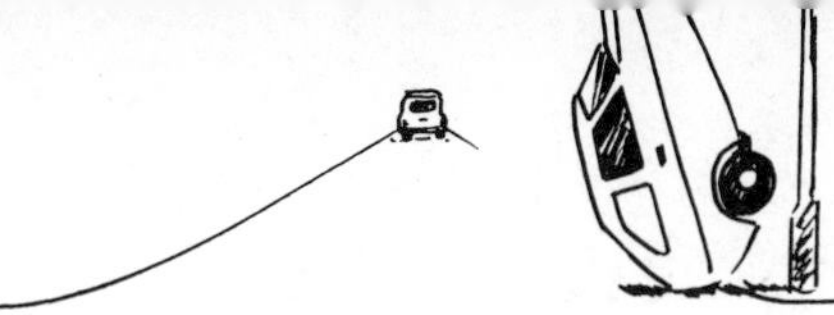

6 Monday

2-6pm Saw!
Saw!
Saw!

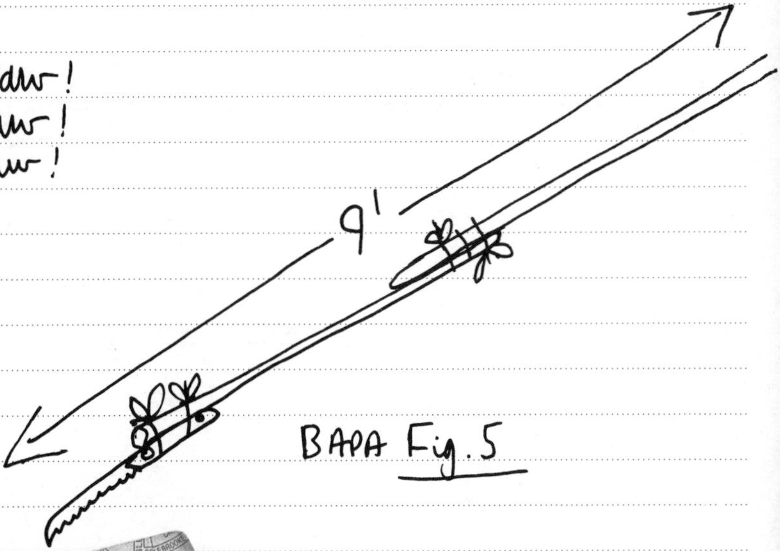

9'

BAPA Fig. 5

7 T:

WANSTEAD

49

WANSTEAD GOLF COUR...

ALDERSBROOK

ALDERSBROOK RD.

LEYTONSTONE

Lift

1,500→
lbs

25 Forward
knots Speed

N
W—E
S

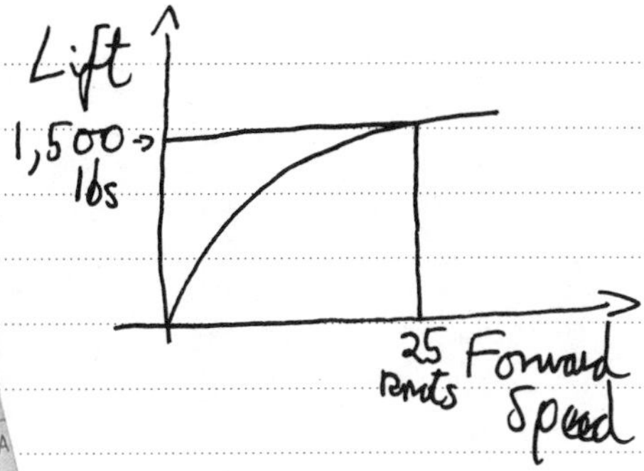

Looking Good
for Mon 13th

September

8 Wednesday

8.30 Biff Biff Biff Screech

11.am Bang bang bang

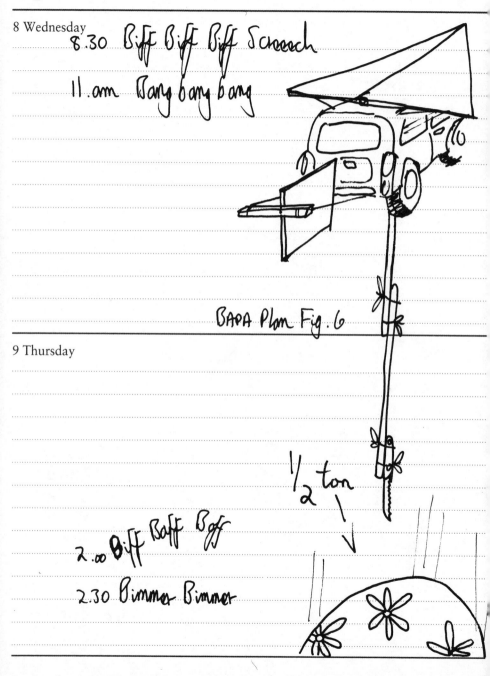

BAPA Plan Fig. 6

---

9 Thursday

½ ton

2.00 Biff Baff Bgff

2.30 Bimmer Bimmer

9 F...

N° 3.

Mr Bean,
I have not slept
for three nights.
If the banging
does not stop I
will call the police.
Maurice N° 3.
(down hall.)

Oh, go away
and sit on a cabbage
(for the rest of your
life)

11 Saturday

Dear God
Oh Lord, who giveth
and taketh away. Giveth me
luck on Monday, but taketh me
not away; unless I do something
really awful like forget to
flush the toilet
Yours sincerely

Mr. Bean

P.S. I hope you are well. I am fine.

12 Sunday

11.15 Church (Pray, pray,
pray)

September

15 Wednesday

Highbury Herald September 15 1993

Bizarre man foiled

A HIGHBURY man's attempt to "put the world to rights" was foiled after police received a tip-off that a lime green mini was about to be launched from the roof of WH Smith in New Road.

The owner of the car, a Mr Bean of Arbor Road, Highbury, was first spotted by pedestrians on the street below, who alerted the police.

"The vehicle in question was fitted with a home-made set of wings, rather like a hang-glider, on the roof," said a police spokesman. "The wings upon inspection seem to have been made from an old bed sheet and some lengths of wood. Also in the car we found a bread knife attached to the end of a broom handle, and an electric fan."

Police are puzzled as Bean's possession of ton of horse

Nagging thought (re. my origins)

4.45 Police Station

11.00 Further questioning.

September

17 Friday

LIE LOW

18 Saturday

LIE LOW

19 Sunday

LIE LOWER

Nº 3.

Dear Mr Bean,
I don't believe
your car was stolen
at all. I saw the
horse dung on the
drive, and I think
you are completely
mad.

Man in Nº 3.
(down hall)

21 Tuesday

I've a funny feeling my
birthday was last Wednesday.

3.

STINK

© BEAN 1993

September

22 Wednesday

NAME Mr. D. Wilkinson
ADDRESS 23A Cherry Lane
London
N.5.
I think your idea is great. Signed.
D. Wilkinson

YIPPEE!!

23 Thursday

9.15 Ring Mr. Wilkinson

4.30 Mr. Wilkinson for tea

Shops: Crumpets   Stodgy cake
       Crusty buns   Lovely cake
       Juicy Cake   + other cake
       Big cake
       Small cake

September

24 Friday

NEW IMPROVED
"SNAIL" RULER

©Mr. Bean

J.00 BANK - get £500
for Mr. Wilkinson

---

25 Saturday

10.00 Drive Mr. Wilkinson
to shops

J.15 Mr. Wilkinson's ointment

---

26 Sunday

10.00 Polish Mr. Wilkinson's
knobs
+knocker

Mr. Wilkinson borrowing
car this afternoon.

10.00 Car due back

September

27 Monday

WHERE IS MR. WILKINSON?

0AM STAB
CUSS WRETCH
DISMEMBER DISEMBOWEL

3.45 Police

WHERE OH WHERE IS MY LOVELY CAR

28 Tuesday

8.40 Catch bus to shops

9.20 Bus

4.30 Smelly bus home again

September

29 Wednesday

Poem: MIND YOUR GRANNY

If there's one thing that's not fetching
It is the sight of someone retching
So at Grandma's please do be extremely careful
If you need to vomit after tea
Then in the toilet you should be
So as not to give your Gran a sticky earful.

Mr. Bean 29 Sept 1993

7.30 Poetry Class

30 Thursday

Possible chorus: Pewky pewky retch retch
Head inside the bowl
Keeping it from Granny
Should be your intended goal.
Tra la

Show to Ms. Rosemary Hosebury

October

1 Friday

WHERE is my £500?

WHERE is my car?

WHERE is slimy puss-y slimbag Mr. Wilkinson?

London Transport
PHOTOCARD

Name of holder
MR/M S

Mr. Bean

Valid for use only by person
shown with a ticket
bearing the same number.

T 5328

2 Saturday

I HATE THE BUSSSS

4 Monday

20,000 ft

"LEMMING BUSES"

© Mr. Bean

5 Tuesday

Plan: 10.00 Catch bus
10.15 Torture bus
11.00 Kill bus

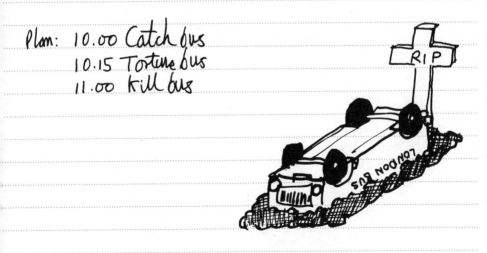

October

Shops: Ace
Celery

7.00 Start Bell Ringing

That revolting couple   ITV (Morning)

9.30 Bell Ringing

8 Friday

1.45am   Bell Ringing

9 Saturday

11.00 More Bell ringing

N°3.

Dear Mr Bean,
Some idiot
keeps ringing
my doorbell
then running
away.
Is it you?

Man in N°3
(down hall).

Hehyhgh
hehhgh
heh!

October

11 Monday

Highbury District Council (Adult Ed. Dept.)
Council Offices
Highbury, London N10

Dear Mr Bean

I am writing on what I know is a very sensitive subject, but I hope you will appreciate my honesty and frankness.

You have been a most enthusiastic pupil at my poetry class, never failing to do your homework and always handing in on time the work which I have requested. I am afraid that I have to tell you, however, that there is something about your work which is really quite shocking, not only to myself, but also to your classmates. They are forced to bear witness to your poetry, as you always insist on reading it out loud during the class, banging the lid of your desk enthusiastically as you do so. As I cannot emphasise enough, we have nothing but admiration for your enthusiasm. But we have had complaints. You may remember that Ann Warburton was physically sick during your stirring rendition of your poem on the same subject (Vomiting), and has never returned. Dear old Derek didn't sleep for a week after the blood-letting trilogy. The class is now half the size it was at the beginning of term, and I'm sorry to say that you and your poetry are the chief cause of the decline in numbers.

Might we interest you in another subject? The Adult Education Institute has over a hundred courses running in the '93-'94 academic year and I am sure we could find one more attuned to your inclinations and enthusiasm. Car maintenance? Italian? I'm sure we could find you something. If you choose to leave our poetry class, we would naturally refund your course fee in full, and also pay the new course's fees for a full five years.

Yours sincerely

Rosemary Hosebury

Rosemary Hosebury (Ms)

Yah boo hiss

*I'm Mr. Dam Bean
Not Mr. Has Bean*

12 Tuesday

*As you might have guessed
You've made me depressed,*

10.15. Buy bottle of alcohol in shop

3 Wednesday

I can do rhymes
Time after time (s)

Whiskey is lovely

French Foreign Legion
010 33 4392 0047

La bla bla

7.30 Poetry Class

TEA
-CHERS

14 Thursday

Ring

Emma

Shirley where are you?
Shirley you understand?

More Gobble Wobble

Wicky

October

Do everything extremely quietly don't make any noise at all I think
this might be what they call a hangover I've read about it in books
move very slowly and speak very very softly do not go out close
curtains sssssssssssshhhh sssssssssssshhh ss s s s sshhh

---

16 Saturday

9.30 Go out quietly
    shopping: Bread
        Ear plugs

12.00 Come in so, so quietly
    Tiptoe upstairs

    SSSSShh

---

17 Sunday

11.15 Don't go to church

8 Monday

4.15 Lemon

9 Tuesday

6.40 CAR RETURNED YIPPEE!

God bless the Highland Police
who returned my car
with its Dayssse (still in it)

2.10 Put music system in car
(needs new stylus)

Records for car: The Very Best of Shirley Bassey
Shirley at her Best
Best of Bassey
Bassey's Best of the Bestest

October

20 Wednesday

Shops: Broom Handles
White sheet

7.30 Poetry Class
8.15 Kendo Class

21 Thursday

Motor Show - Earl's Court

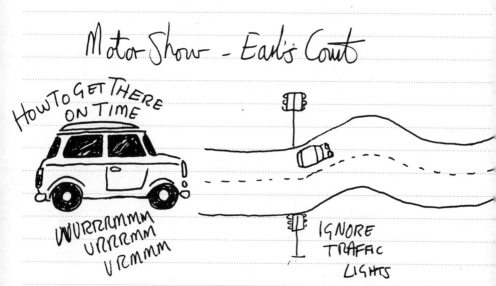

HOW TO GET THERE ON TIME

WURRRMMM
URRRMM
VRMMM

IGNORE TRAFIC LIGHTS

2 Friday

110 MPH SAFE

SCREECH!

EP
EEP

APPROACH PEDESTRIAN CROSSING:
1. HORN
2. ACCELERATE
3. CLOSE EYES

SQUEAL!

Saturday

24 Sunday

CHILDREN'S
PLAYGROUND

HUMP
BACKED BRIDGE

PEDESTRIAN

PRECINCT

TRAFFIC
JAM
(TAKE
SHORT
CUT)

October

Petrol
Lettuce
Stamps

I thought girls
Always had curls

HAY
STACK →

85 mph SAFE

WET ROAD:
1. ACCELERATE
2. SWERVE FROM
   SIDE TO SIDE

ROUNDABOUT:
GO ROUND 3 TIMES
FLAT OUT

7 Wednesday

WARP SPEED

ROAD
NARROWS

RELIANT
ROBIN

POLICE
← CAR

NA NUR!
NA NUR!

OUT

8.15 Kondo Class

8 Thursday

Plan: 8.15 Go to Japan

12.30 Have lunch

Not possible

4.00 Come home

October

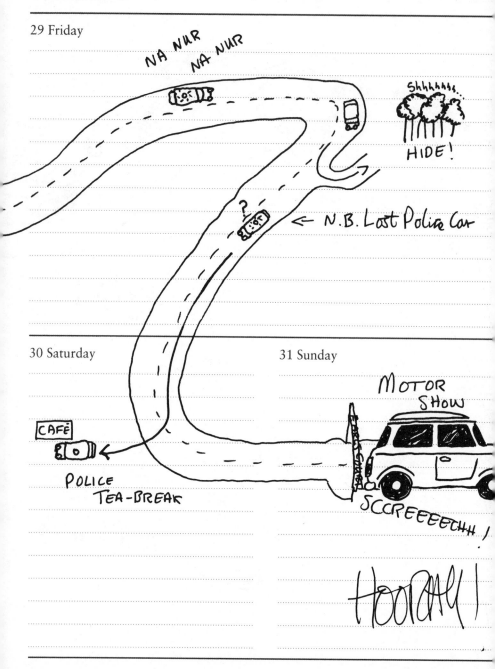

Monday

Oven broken — [Ring Gas Man]

Buy salad stuff: Tomatoes
Cucumber
Weeds
Insects
Soil

Dinner: Salad & Bread

Tuesday

9.00 Gas Man

12.00 Oven still broken

Lunch: Salad   stupid STUPID

Gas Man

Dinner: Salad

November

3 Wednesday

I HATE SALAD

Gas Ma[r...]

8.15: Try and cook without oven (Lamb chops)

9.00: FIRE BRIGADE

2.45am Sleep.

4 Thursday

9.00 Shops: ~~Flower~~ Flour × 30 lbs
Eggs

Plot plot plot plot plot

November

Friday → Guy Fawkes Night

plot plot plot plot plot

ipping
ous Clippers!)
treason
plot treason plot treason plot treason plot X

8pm. Bonfire Party (in Park)

GET THEM WITH FLOUR BOMB
(then throw eggs)
if time

Saturday

9.00 Police station
Questioning

all day

7 Sunday

Fireworks Fright

POLICE WERE CALLED to a bonfire party last night where a man was apprehended under suspicion of intending to plant a large explosive on the bonfire. "What we suspected of being a large bomb turned out to be a bag of flour and eggs", said event organiser Don Haze. "When I dragged him out of the tree he told me he was just about to make a cake."

Mr Bean, of Arbor Road, London, was detained at local

November

8 Monday

"COMMON SENSE"

© Mr. Bean

9 Tuesday

1.00 Egg

7.00 Another egg

METROPOLITAN POLICE
RECEIPT

your ref:

our ref:

Surrendered Goods

2 BROOM HANDLES

P.C. R. Leaws

The above items have been confiscated pending
a decision by local magistrates

8.15
Mick's Kendo Club

Challenge Mick
to DUEL

5.15 Duel at Dawn

Requirements: Broom handle
Sheet

Report: 4.45 Hospital (neck brace)
6.00 Police (re. broom handles)

November

12 Friday

4.15 Stake out

WHAT!

Plan

13 Saturday

14 Sunday

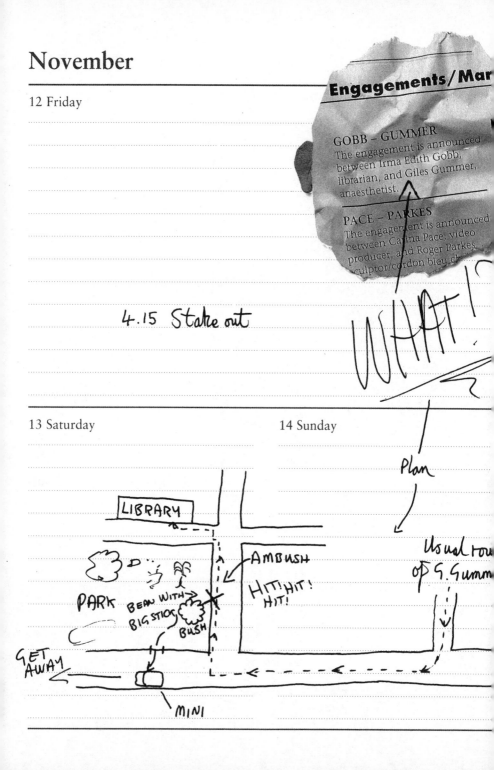

LIBRARY

PARK

BEAN WITH
BIG STICK

BUSH

AMBUSH

HIT! HIT!
HIT!

GET
AWAY

MINI

Usual rou
of G. Gumm

5 Monday

SHIRLEY BASSEY LETTER

ν. ν. ν. ν. ν. ν. ν. ν. ν. ν. ν. ν. important

4.10 POST BOX

6 Tuesday

If I was going to choose a day
I would choose Choose-day.

4.07 Gummer Ambush   POLICE SUSPICIOUS

HIDE DIARY

GUMMER 2

STRETCH   J.   TUG

November

17 Wednesday

HIDE DIARY

12.15 POLICE CALLING ROUND.

N.B. COUNTRY DANCING   8.15 Andris Karods Club   Meet Monday

18 Thursday

TOAST RECIPE

Burn Bread
Eat

Shirley Bassey
Entertainments

Las Vegas • Hollywood • Monte Carlo • London

Mr Bean
c/o Mrs Wickets
"Daffodils"
Room 2
12 Arbor Road
London N10

Dear Mr Bean

Thank you for your recent letter to Ms Bassey; I'm sorry I've been so
late in replying.

I am sorry to say that the vocal microphones used by Ms Bassey
during her performances are extremely expensive items, and it would
be impossible to send them as souvenirs to fans who request them.

Enclosed is a signed photograph as partial compensation!

Yours sincerely

Richard Kershaw

Richard Kershaw
Technical Manager
Shirley Bassey Ents.

*Write
again*

November

22 Monday

START→

1 — 2 Tum TeeTum Tra la la

7:00 Country Dancing

23 Tuesday

Jump

AIRBORNE

TWIST

(Turn) Tra la-la -te tum tum tiddle tiddle

4 Wednesday

Boff Boff

um Bang
Bang

Trrrrumm

Titty

Deedee
Deedee
Dee

Voopp!

5 Thursday

Skip

Hop

La — la — la

teedly — dee Bink Bink Boodle Baff

FINISH

November

2.00
Shoes
Honey

Shirley Bassey
Entertainments

Las Vegas · Hollywood · Monte Carlo · London

Mr Bean
c/o Mrs Wickets
"Daffodils"
Room 2
12 Arbor Road
London N10

Dear Mr Bean

I acknowledge receipt of your letter of the 17th of July.

I understand that we misread the request in your last letter, and that there was no grammatical error. Your request was to BE one of Ms Bassey's microphones, rather than to posses one.

I should warn you that, in accordance with the policy of this office, your letter has been passed to the police.

Yours sincerely

Adrian Silverman
for Shirley Bassey Ents.

November

29 Monday — Mrs. Wicket going to Bournemouth

Look after Kipper

KIPPER

Please look after
Kipper. He is
very sensitive and
needs feeding
every day
Mrs Wicket

7.00
Country Dancing
Tra-la-la-dee-dum-te-tum

1-21-21-21-2 and rest.

25 days to Christmas

December

N° 3.

Dear Mr Bean,
Have you heard
that barking from
Mrs Wicket's?

Man in N° 3.
(down hall).

It is you that's
barking!

Nagging thought

2 Thursday

Nagging thought

Friday

Nagging thought

---

4 Saturday

8.00 Nagging tho

oh my God NO

AAAARGHH

12 MIDNIGHT: Put Kipper's corpse in middle of road
(Act natural)

---

5 Sunday

MRS. WICKET BACK
FROM BOURNEMOUTH

Dear Mrs. Wicket
I was so sorry to hear that Kipper had escaped and been run over while my back was turned. I think I was ironing at the time, although I did hear brakes and, thinking it was a bat screeching sub-sonically,

December

6 Monday

11am Funeral (Kipper)

THINKS

1.15 Sink blocked

7 Tuesday

Ring Madame Sandra

2.00 Madame Sandra

No luck

December

Wednesday

1.00 Madame Sandra
    (Some progress)

Mum's ghost?

Madame Sandra

Thursday

11.45 Madame Sandra

MADE CONTACT WITH Mum

    Question: Where is the plunger for the sink?
    Answer: Under the stairs

12.10 Unblock sink ✓

December

10 Friday

1.00 Crisps

11 Saturday

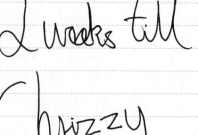

2 weeks till
Chrizzy

12 Sunday

December

13 Monday

9.15 Madame Sandra
   (Talk to Charles Dickens)

          Q: What was supposed to
             happen to Edwin Drood?

          A: Hadn't made up his mind.

14 Tuesday

                          ← more respectful

Dear ~~Santa~~ Mr. Claus,
                    I hope you are well. I am fine.
There really is not very long to ~~go~~ now until Christmas, so I
~~thought~~ I might write ~~and~~ with a provisional list of presents
~~order of preference~~:

          1. A quantity of High Explosive
                    (Semtex, or equivalent)
          2. Small rubber fork.
          3. New mother
          4. Brass hook   (Toilet door)
          5. t.b.a.

December

10.00 Buy New TV

+ Radio Times
TV Times
~~Financial Times~~
TV Quick

QUICK!

NEW ROOM PLANS FOR CHRISTMAS
(TO ACCOMODATE TV)

DOOR

WINDOW

TV

BED

WINDOW

CHAIR

CHAIR

DOOR

WINDOW

(LOTS OF SPACE)

WINDOW

BED

1 Week till

Chrizzzy

DOOR

CHAIR

TV

BRACKET

(EVEN MORE SPACE)

BED

December

20 Monday

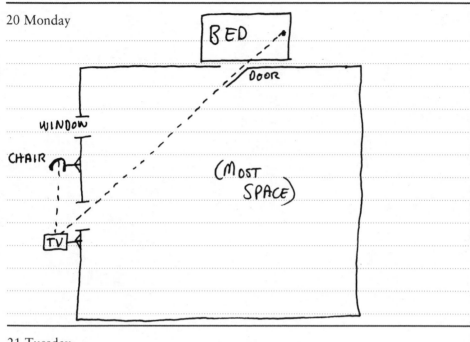

21 Tuesday

("Daffodils")

Dear Mr. Claus

I hope you are well. I am fine. Only four days till the birthday of our Lord Jesus Christ, and I've had a change of heart: I would now like a Drum Kit which I can bash and bash and bash

New order
1. Snare drum   5. Tom-Tom
2. Cymbal   6. "   "
3. Bass drum   7. "   "
4. Tom-Tom   8. Brass hook (TOILET DOOR)
4a. Hi-hat   9.

22. Santa xx

December

2 Wednesday

POST LETTER TO SANTA

DRUM PRACTICE:

ght hand	Tink Tink Tink Tink Tink Tink Tink Tink Tink Tink
ft hand	Chap Chap Chap Chap Chap
ht Foot	Boom BoomBoom Boom BoomBoom Boom
ft Foot	Chish Chish

3 Thursday

Santa should get letter ~~this letter~~ this morning

Try: Biddley Biddley Biddley
L R L   R L R   L R L

Biddley phoomp titty
L R L   F   R R

bash bash
L   L

EXCITING EXCITING
EXCITING
EXCITING EXCITING

If I get a drum kit
I'm going to go mad

December

24 Friday

I want a drum kit
I want a drum kit
Tiddle diddle rapple rapple
Bum Boom tish.

Shops: Buy cracker

Buy brass hook.

25 Saturday   Christmas Day

26 Sunday

OOOh! BRASS HOOK for
Christmas!

Just what I NEED!!

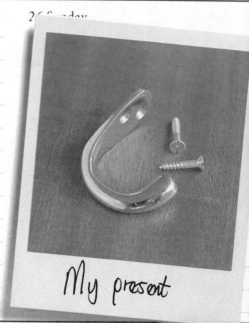

My present

No other presents

(Cracker didn't crack — send back to man)

7 Monday   Boxing Day

10.00 Go to Park   (empty)

Practise on
drum kit

No shops open

Evening: stay in

8 Tuesday

Water plant   (in next door garden)

Practise on drum
kit

I don't like Christmas very much if I had to be honest

December

29 Wednesday

Practise on drum kit

Shops: Bread
Hazelnut
Tangerine?

30 Thursday

9.00 Bird Watching

COMMON WADER

BACK

FRONT

TAKING OFF

SIDE

IN FLIGHT

7.00 Common Wader
(Gas Mark 7
2-2½ hrs.)

1 Friday

New Year Resolutions

1.
2.
3. Tidy room
4.

~~Marriage~~

Can't think of anything

Saturday

GRAND new-YEAR
clean and sparkling and shiney

1994
GLEAM
SPARKLE

2 Sunday

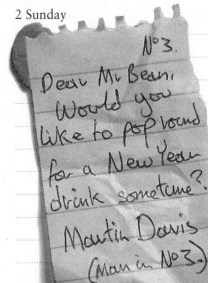

Nº3.

Dear Mr Bean,
Would you
like to pop round
for a New Year
drink sometime?
Martin Davis.
(Man in Nº 3.)

P.T.O ⇒

1994 Year Planner

	January	February	March	April	May	June
Mon						
Tue		1	1			
Wed		2	2			1
Thu		3				2
Fri		4				3
Sat	1					4
Sun	2				1	5
Mon	3*				2*	6*
Tue	4*				3	7
Wed	5				4	8
Thu	6				5	9
Fri	7				6	10
Sat	8				7	11
Sun	9				8	12
Mon	10				9	13
Tue	11				10	14
Wed	12				11	15
Thu	13				12	16
Fri	14				13	17
Sat	15				14	18
Sun	16				15	19
Mon	17			18	16	20
Tue	18	22		19	17	21
Wed	19	23	23	20	18	22
Thu	20	24	24	21	19	23
Fri	21	25	25	22	20	24
Sat	22	26	26	23	21	25
Sun	23	27	27	24	22	26
Mon	24	28	28	25	23	27
Tue	25		29	26	24	28
Wed	26		30	27	25	29
Thu	27		31	28	26	30
Fri	28			29	27	
Sat	29			30	28	
Sun	30				29	
Mon	31				30*	
Tue					31	

BURY HATCHET

	January	February	March	April	May	June

January	March	April	May	June
3 UK, R of Ireland	17 Ireland (N & R)	1 UK, R of Ireland	2 UK	6 R of Ireland
4 Scotland		4 England, Ireland (N & R), Wales	30 UK	

1994 Year Planner

July	August	September	October	November	December
	1*				
	2			1	
	3			2	
	4	1		3	1
1	5	2		4	2
2	6	3	1	5	3
3	7	4	2	6	4
4	8	5	3	7	5
5	9	6	4	8	6
6	10	7	5	9	7
7	11	8	6	10	8
8	12	9	7	11	9
9	13	10	8	12	10
10	14	11	9	13	11
11	15	12	10	14	12
12*	16	13	11	15	13
13	17	14	12	16	14
14	18	15	13	17	15
15	19	16	14	18	16
16	20	17 10.00 SEX	15	19	17
17	21	18 CHANGE?	16	20	18
18	22	19 (Dr. Lahote)	17	21	19
19	23	20	18	22	20
20	24	21	19	23	21
21	25	22	20	24	22
22	26	23	21	25	23
23	27	24	22	26	24
24	28	25	23	27	25
25	29*	26	24	28	26*
26	30	27	25	29	27*
27	31	28	26	30	28
28		29	27		29
29		30	28		30
30			29		31
31			30		
			31*		

July	August	September	October	November	December
12 N Ireland	1 R of Ireland, Scotland 29 England, N Ireland Wales	3 R of Irelland			26 UK, R of Ireland 27 UK, R of Ireland

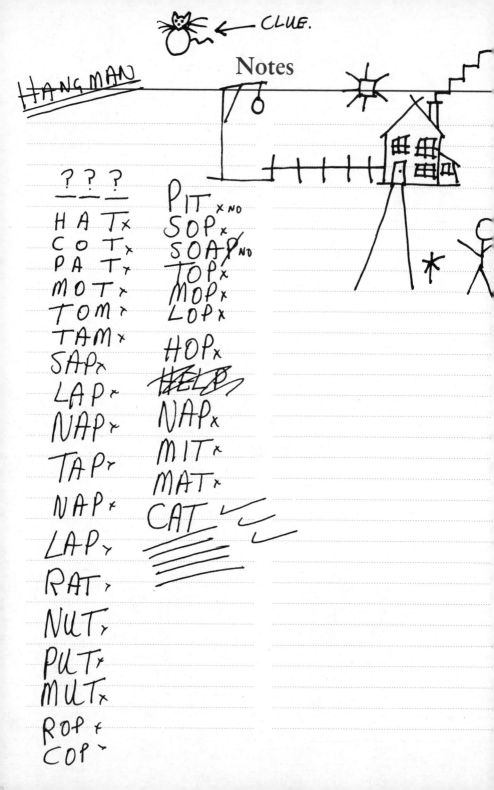

Chadwell School for Boys

Term: SUMMER TERM, 1971   Name: ⬛EAN

Subject	Mark	Comments	
History	35%	He has no sense of history. But then, of course, he has no sense.	T.A.P.R
Chemistry	53%	He is inventive. As a result, form 5B is lucky to be alive.	T.A.B
Mathematics	94%	An obnoxious, self-satisfied, self-centred, shabby, dribbling, bone-idle, toadying cow-pat of a pupil; his most revolting quality being that he is quite, quite brilliant.	M.J.L
Physics	65%	Very encouraging. A boy died when co-operating with my lie-detector experiment, as you know, but nevertheless the exam results are excellent.	Mr Hutt
Geography	54%	A surprisingly good result considering he only succeeded in finding the classroom twice this term	K.W.
Biology	41%	He really has no idea, but then hopefully he will never breed.	P.A.B.
Religious Knowledge	25%	No progress this year, sadly. He once claimed that he worshipped the God of Lemonade which rather confused us all, I'm afraid.	N.N
Art	58%	He draws well, but has difficulty with nudes (looking at them).	P.B.

Good luck. He'll need it. S Love

Headmaster

© Mr. Bean 1993

Notes

PLAN

→ 1. Photocopy this × 10 million

(Joanis Copyshop
105 lip U st.)

then 2.

it.

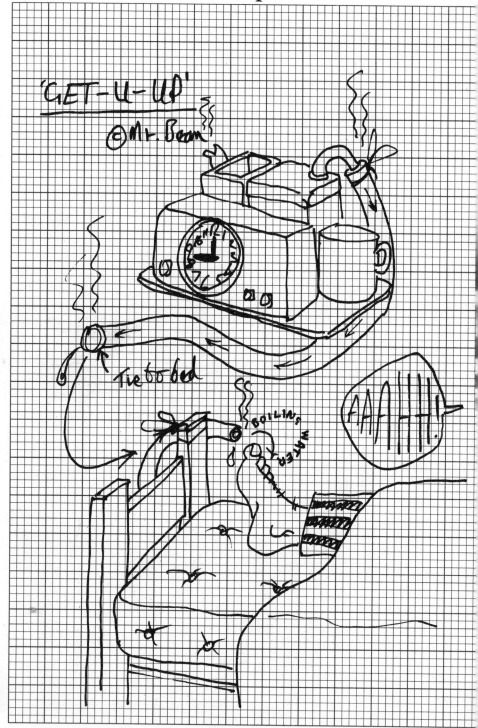

Graph

Holes

'EYEBATH'
© Mr. Bean

EYE WASH

FIT TO TAP

Mine! Mine! Mine!

'SNOWSHOE'
© Mr. Bean

£3m. for a cup o' tea guv?

Lucky George Wilkinson, of no fixed abode, landed more than the price of a cuppa when Littlewoods coughed up a record £3,000,000 yesterday.

"I'm over the moon," he told our reporter. "Three months ago I lost my last £500 on a racehorse and have been sleeping rough ever since." George, 63, said that winning the pools will not change him except that after rubbing shoulders with some of "Britain's grubbiest" he might just start mixing with a better class of person.

"The fir st thing I'm go...